This Little Tiger book belongs to:

_____

_____

_____

For Rala – P B

To Chris, Sally, Maya and Gabriel – J C

LITTLE TIGER PRESS
1 The Coda Centre, 189 Munster Road, London SW6 6AW
www.littletiger.co.uk
First published in Great Britain 2011
This edition published 2011
Text copyright © Paul Bright 2011
Illustrations copyright © Jane Chapman 2011
Visit Jane Chapman at www.ChapmanandWarnes.com
Paul Bright and Jane Chapman have asserted their rights to be
identified as the author and illustrator of this work under the Copyright,
Designs and Patents Act, 1988 • A CIP catalogue record for this book is
available from the British Library • All rights reserved
ISBN: 978-1-84895-236-2
LTP/1900/0883/0314
Printed in China
4 6 8 10 9 7 5 3

The Not-So Scary Snorklum

Paul Bright

Jane Chapman

LITTLE TIGER PRESS
London

The setting sun glowed orange as the scary
Snorklum stomped home to his cave on the hill.
"I'm late!" he thought, and his
whiskers began to wibble in a worried
sort of way.

Then he met Mole, and although his
head told him he was late, his tummy
told him he was hungry.

"I AM THE SCARY SNORKLUM," he growled, "and I am going to have Mole sandwich for tea, with a little salt and pepper and chunky pickle."

"If you are the scary Snorklum," said
Mole, "why are you wibbling in
your whiskers in a worried sort of way?"
  "Whiskers wibbling?" snorted
the Snorklum. "Worried? What nonsense!
Nothing worries a Snorklum!"
  He put Mole in his pocket to eat
later and hurried on his way.

The sinking sun glowed red as the scary
Snorklum hurried onwards up the hill.
"I must be home by dark," he
muttered, and his tail began to twitch
in a timid sort of way.

Then he met Rabbit, and although his head told him he was very late, his tummy told him that a Rabbit pie would be even better than a Mole sandwich.

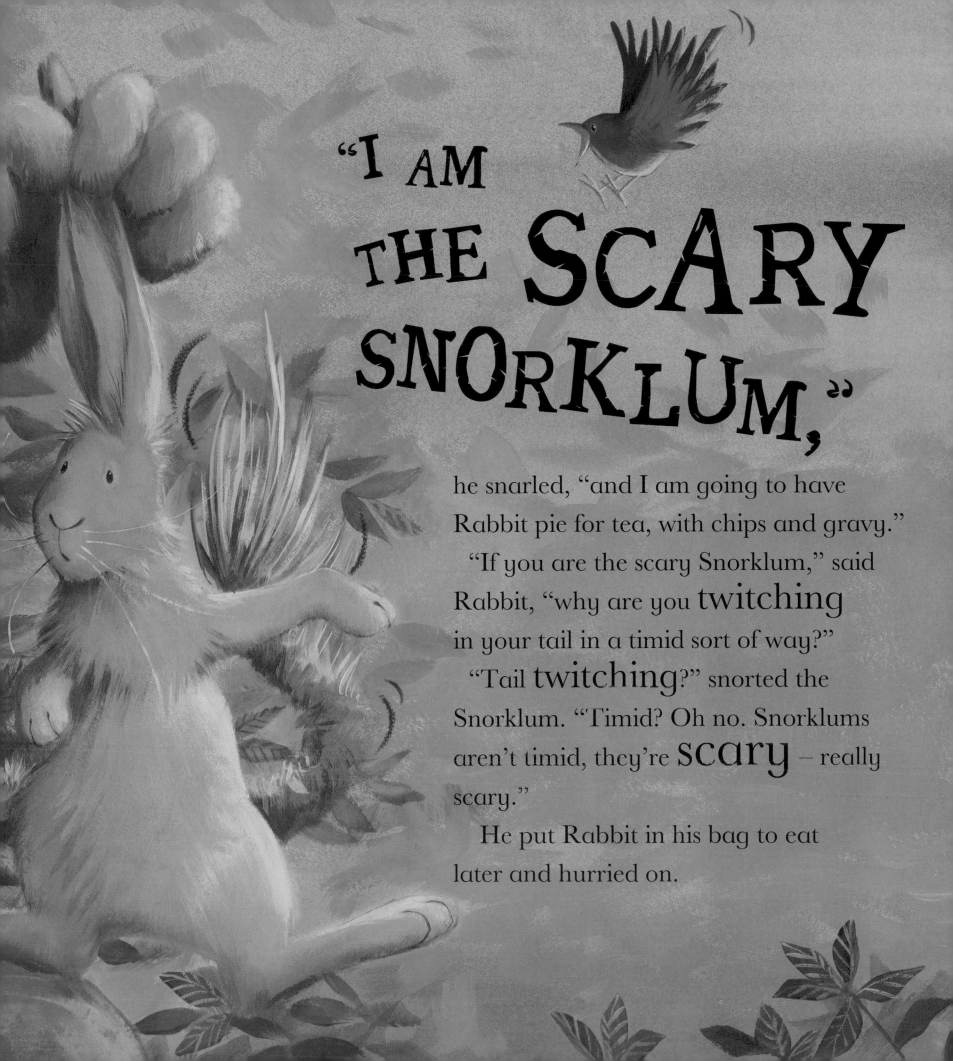

"I AM THE SCARY SNORKLUM,"

he snarled, "and I am going to have Rabbit pie for tea, with chips and gravy."

"If you are the scary Snorklum," said Rabbit, "why are you twitching in your tail in a timid sort of way?"

"Tail twitching?" snorted the Snorklum. "Timid? Oh no. Snorklums aren't timid, they're scary – really scary."

He put Rabbit in his bag to eat later and hurried on.

The sun dipped and disappeared as
the scary Snorklum raced up the hill.
"I am SO late," he gasped. "I must
be home by night-time!" And his knees
began to knock in a nervous sort
of way.

Then he met Badger, and although his head told him that he was **very**, very late, his tummy told him that a Badger stew would be even tastier than a Rabbit pie.

"I AM THE SCARY SNORKLUM," he roared, "and I am going to have Badger stew for tea, with peas and dumplings."

"If you really are the scary Snorklum," said Badger, "why are you knocking in your knees?"

"And twitching in your tail?" said Rabbit.

"And wibbling in your whiskers?" added Mole. "Are you a scary Snorklum or . . .

a scared Snorklum?"

"Or maybe," said Badger, "you're
not a Snorklum at all!"

"Of course I am a Snorklum!" bellowed the
Snorklum, quite forgetting that he was in a hurry.
"I can prove it! And when I'm done . . .

I WILL EAT YOU ALL FOR TEA!"

"I have heard," said Badger, "that a scary Snorklum can scare the leaves off of the trees, with a single stare."

"I can do that," said the Snorklum. "Just you watch." He screwed up his face and he stared and stared.

The trees shook and shivered,

and their leaves fell, fluttering,

to the ground.

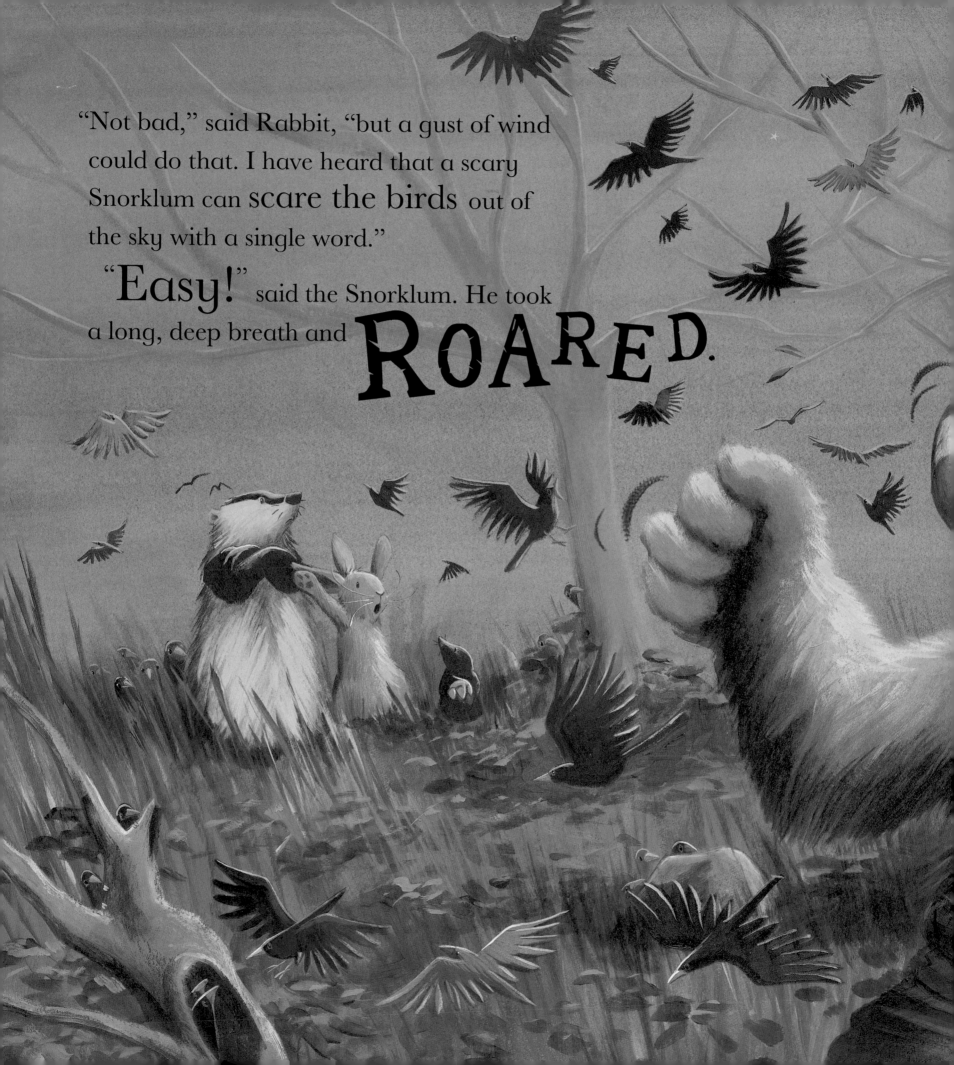

"Not bad," said Rabbit, "but a gust of wind could do that. I have heard that a scary Snorklum can scare the birds out of the sky with a single word."

"Easy!" said the Snorklum. He took a long, deep breath and ROARED.

The birds all flew down
from the sky and hid in the
trees and bushes, trembling.

"But the birds settle in the trees at night anyway," said Mole. "And you **can't be a scary Snorklum**, because I have heard that if a scary Snorklum stays out **after dark** he goes . . ."

As darkness finally fell the scary Snorklum – for he really was **a scary Snorklum** – shrunk, with a POOFFT! and a flash and a cry, into a tiny, timid Snorklum.

"You tricked me!" he squeaked.

"But when I've grown big and scary

again, I'll be back! And next time,

I'll have YOU for
breakfast!"

Pick up more exciting books from Little Tiger Press!

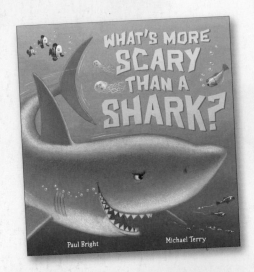
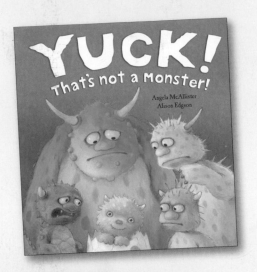

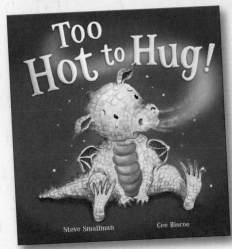